Whispers of Discord, Songs of Harmony

The Nexus Project Saga Begins

SANDEEP RAVIDAS

Dedication

To the dreamers and believers, whose
imaginations know no bounds.

For those who find solace in the pages of a book,
where realms of magic unfold and heroes rise.

To the ones who seek echoes of eternity in the
whispers of the wind and the rustle of leaves.

May the enchantment within these pages kindle
the flame of your own adventurous spirit.

This tale is dedicated to those who dare to
envision a world beyond the veil, where the
echoes of eternity resonate in the hearts of those
who believe in the magic of possibility.

May your dreams forever dance among the stars.

With gratitude and magic,

Preface

In the twilight of imagination and the realms where dreams intertwine with reality, "Whispers of Power: Chronicles of Lumina Unleashed" beckons you into a world where magic flows like a river and destiny is inscribed in the stars. Within these pages, the story of Lumina continues, now unfurling its wings in a journey of power, revelation, and the echoes of eternity.

As we delve into this unfolding saga, brace yourself for a symphony of enchanted landscapes, where the very fabric of Lumina trembles with secrets and the allure of the unknown. Our journey takes us beyond the Veil, where echoes of power linger, waiting to be discovered by those with the courage to listen.

Lumina, a realm bound by the threads of fate, is once again at the mercy of forces unseen. The characters you will meet are not mere players in this grand tapestry; they are the architects of Lumina's destiny. The enchantress Elara, the elven archer, the sorcerer, the mysterious rogue, and the gentle giant—all bound by a shared purpose that transcends time and space.

The echoes within these pages are not just words; they are the harmonies of Lumina's very soul. As we embark on this journey together, may you feel the whispers of power seeping through the parchment, igniting the spark of imagination within your own being.

So, dear reader, brace yourself for an odyssey of magic, mystery, and moments that resonate with the timeless echoes of power. Lumina awaits, and the adventure is about to begin.

Welcome to a world where whispers hold the key to unlocking the true potential within. The Chronicles of Lumina are about to be unleashed.

Acknowledgements

I extend my heartfelt gratitude to the countless dreamers and storytellers who have inspired the creation of "Whispers of Eldoria." This journey would not have been possible without the support, creativity, and magic shared by those who believe in the power of storytelling.

CHAPTER ONE

The Hidden Portal

Sunlight, the shade of honey, dripped through the emerald cover of the Enchanted woodland, casting dappled styles on the moss-carpeted earth. Rachel, her backpack laden with the spoils of a protracted day's exploration, pushed via the undergrowth, her brow furrowed in concentration. no matter the idyllic beauty surrounding her, she wasn't there to recognize the surroundings. She turned into on a project.

driven by means of a lifelong fascination with historical civilizations, Rachel had dedicated her profession to unearthing hidden truths. today, her quest led her deep into the uncharted coronary heart of the wooded area, following cryptic clues on a weathered parchment map. The map, discovered in a dusty antique store, talked about a mythical portal leading to Eldoria, a mythical realm untouched by time. most disregarded it as mere delusion, but Rachel, along with her insatiable interest and unwavering notion within the impossible, saw it as a challenge.

Her heart hammered with anticipation as she emerged right into a clearing bathed in an eerie, blue-tinged light. within the middle stood a monolithic structure, in contrast to whatever she had ever visible. Carved from an unknown, obsidian-like material, it pulsed with an inner light, its surface etched with swirling symbols that appeared to writhe and dance before her eyes. This was it. The portal.

With trembling palms, Rachel extracted the final artifact from her bag – a tarnished silver key engraved with the same swirling symbols. As she slotted it into a keyhole at the portal's surface, the clearing hummed with strength. The symbols blazed with mild, forming a swirling vortex. a gasp escaped Rachel's lips. This turned into no mere legend; this changed into real.

The hum crescendoed, enveloping her in a dazzling mild. Panic threatened to devour her, however the archaeologist in her wouldn't allow it. Taking a deep breath, she advanced, disappearing into the heart of the swirling vortex.

the sector dissolved into a kaleidoscope of colors, the familiar woodland replaced by a whirlwind of impossibilities. while the lighting subsided, Rachel located herself standing on soft, verdant grass below a sky painted with two moons. Towering trees, taller than any she'd ever seen, stretched in the direction of the heavens, their leaves shimmering with an otherworldly glow. atypical, melodious chirps filled the air, and inside the distance, the faint shimmer of a waterfall promised hidden wonders.

This become Eldoria. reality bent to its very own regulations right here, in which magic whispered within the rustling leaves and creatures of fable may want to stroll the earth. A thrill of fear and pleasure coursed through Rachel's veins. getting into the unknown, she embarked on a journey that would project everything she thought she knew, rewriting now not simply history books, but the very cloth of her very own existence.

The Whispers of Eldoria

Emboldened by the breathtaking panorama earlier than her, Rachel cautiously ventured deeper into the woodland. The air held a tang of magic, sweet and overseas, not like whatever she'd ever skilled. glowing butterflies, the dimensions of her hand, flitted around her, their wings casting an airy glow at the forest floor. odd, musical calls echoed thru the bushes, reputedly beckoning her ahead.

unexpectedly, a flash of motion caught her eye. A creature not like any she'd visible in her textbooks sprang from in the back of a tree. It resembled a deer, but its fur shimmered with iridescent shades, and its antlers glowed with an inner light. The creature, seemingly unafraid, fixated its big, shrewd eyes on Rachel, tilting its head inquisitively.

Rachel, hesitant before everything, reduced her backpack and held out a hand. To her surprise, the creature nudged her palm with its soft nostril, emitting a gentle trill. A feel of calm washed over her, dispelling the preliminary fear. perhaps the magic of Eldoria prolonged even to its inhabitants.

Following the creature, Rachel delved deeper into the forest, drawn with the aid of an insatiable interest. The course led her to a babbling brook, its water shimmering with an ethereal mild. As she knelt to take a sip, a voice, gentle and melodic, whispered through the leaves.

"Welcome, stranger, to the world of Eldoria."

Rachel's coronary heart skipped a beat. She spun round, attempting to find the supply of the voice, but saw not anything however swaying leaves and flitting butterflies.

"Do not be afraid," the voice endured, apparently emanating from anywhere and nowhere right now. "i'm Sylvana, guardian of the forest. who are you, and what brings you to our land?"

Rachel, nevertheless awestruck, defined her adventure, the artifact, and her look for the legendary Eldoria. Sylvana listened patiently, her voice laced with amusement.

"you're the first outsider to attain Eldoria in generations," Sylvana said. "Our realm has long been hidden from the eyes of mortals, for magic prospers satisfactory while undisturbed."

Rachel felt a pang of guilt. Had she trespassed with the aid of entering this world?

"Do no longer fret," Sylvana soothed. "Your arrival turned into foreseen. The artifact you possess became entrusted to you for a motive."

Sylvana went on to provide an explanation for that Eldoria turned into dealing with a grave risk, a darkness creeping from the fringes in their realm, threatening to devour all that become lovely and magical. The artifact, the key of Eldoria, turned into part of an ancient protection mechanism, and Rachel, chosen via fate, turned into destined to play a vital function in saving their international.

overwhelmed via the burden of this revelation, Rachel hesitated. "but i am simply an archaeologist," she protested. "What can i do in opposition to such darkness?"

Sylvana smiled enigmatically. "more than you realize, young one. The magic of Eldoria flows inside you, ready to be awakened. however your adventure has just started. There are others who watch for you, folks that hold the understanding and power to fight the encroaching darkness. Are you geared up to embrace your future?"

Rachel checked out the important thing of Eldoria clutched in her hand, her coronary heart pounding with a mixture of fear and exhilaration. This turned into no everyday archaeological expedition; it turned into a name to journey, a fight for the fate of a whole international. With a newfound willpower, she met Sylvana's gaze.

"i am geared up," she declared, her voice echoing through the ancient woodland.

for that reason began Rachel's exceptional adventure in Eldoria, a realm where reality and myth interlaced, and her personal ability awaited to be unlocked. Little did she know, the direction ahead would be fraught with risk, filled with each legendary allies and ambitious foes. but with the important thing of Eldoria in her hand and the whispers of magic guiding her, Rachel become determined to upward push to the challenge and guard the wonders of Eldoria, even supposing it supposed rewriting her personal destiny.

The Whispers Lead On

Guided by Sylvanas' ethereal whisper, Rachel emerged from the forest's emerald embrace onto a sunlit plain. Before her stretched rolling hills dotted with wildflowers in hues never seen on Earth, while in the distance majestic waterfalls cascaded from crystal cliffs. It was a breathtaking landscape, yet the weight of Sylvanas' words hung heavy in the air.

Suddenly, a melodious chorus filled the air, drawing Rachel's attention to a group of figures approaching from the horizon. They moved with otherworldly grace, their forms shimmering with the same iridescent glow as deer in the forest. As they approached, Rachel recognized them as Sylphs, winged creatures with translucent skin and hair that flowed like spun moonlight. Their leader, a woman with eyes like pools of starlight, introduced herself as Lumina, the Dreamweaver.

Lumina explained that they were summoned by Sylvanas because Rachel's journey required not only courage, but also knowledge and guidance. With gentle smiles and voices like tinkling bells, the Sylphs led Rachel to a hidden grove where an ancient tree stood silent guardian, its branches heavy with glittering leaves. An older elf waited beneath his canopy, his face etched with time and wisdom.

Elara, Keeper of Memories, greeted Rachel with a knowing smile. He spoke of an ancient prophecy, of a mortal destined to wield the Key of Eldoria and unite the various races of Eldoria against the encroaching darkness. He revealed that the darkness stems from a damaged artifact, the Shadowshard, lost for centuries but now stirring and threatening to engulf the realm in eternal night.

With each revelation, Rachel's initial apprehension turned to steely determination. Elara presented her with a map etched in moonstone, the surface of which revealed hidden paths and forgotten cities, each containing a fragment of the Key's power that needed to be collected. He warned her of dangerous trials and cunning guardians, each testing her mettle and unlocking the magic within.

Bidding farewell to the ethereal beings, Rachel embarked on her perilous quest. Armed with a map, a key, and a growing sense of purpose, she set out into the heart of Eldoria. Sylvanas' whispers guided her steps, guiding her through hidden valleys and past watchful stone giants. She encountered mischievous Goblins who tested her wits, traversed treacherous caves guarded by fire-breathing dragons, and befriended a grumpy but loyal Gnome named Bramble who served as her reluctant guide.

Every challenge she overcame, every shard of the Key's power she gained felt like a step closer to fulfilling the prophecy. However, with each victory, the shadow of the growing darkness grew larger. News reached her of villages destroyed and creatures corrupted by the influence of the Shadow. Eldoria's whisper became urgent, begging her to hasten her journey.

As Rachel progressed deeper into the realm, the lines between reality and fantasy blurred. She witnessed talking trees sharing ancient secrets, witnessed constellations come to life at night, and danced with fireflies that painted the twilight in shimmering patterns. In this wonderland, she not only discovered a hidden potential within herself, but also a connection to the magic of Eldoria that ran deeper than she could have ever imagined.

But even as she thrived in her adventure, the weight of her responsibility weighed heavily. On her shoulders rested the fate of a world she barely knew, a daunting task for a mere archaeologist. Still, fueled by a whisper of hope and the courage that ignited within her, Rachel continued, determined to face the darkness and rewrite her own destiny hand in hand with the magic of Eldoria.

The Gathering Storm

As Rachel sank deeper into Eldoria, the whispers of the earth grew louder, painting a grim picture of impending doom. The Shadow's influence spread like a creeping darkness, corrupting everything it touched. Villages lay in ruins, their inhabitants either driven away or twisted into monstrous shadows of their former selves.

Rachel's resolve hardened with each step. She saw the beauty and wonder of Eldoria and did not allow the darkness to consume her. But the task before her was daunting. The shadow was powerful, its tendrils reaching into every corner of the realm. To beat it, she would need all the help she could get.

Fortunately, she wasn't alone. Along her journey, she gathers a group of loyal companions: Bramble, a grumpy but well-informed Gnome; Lumina, the wise and gentle Sylph; and Kael, a fierce and skilled elven warrior. Together they form an unlikely but formidable team, united by their determination to save Eldoria.

Their journey took them to the far corners of the realm, from the frozen peaks of the Frostfang Mountains to the hot sands of the Scorched Desert. They faced countless dangers, from bloodthirsty goblins to wily trolls to twisted creatures corrupted by Stínohard. But with each challenge they overcame, their bond grew stronger and their belief in their mission never wavered.

Finally, after many trials and tribulations, they reached the lair of the Shadowshard, a dark and twisted fortress hidden deep in the heart of Eldoria. The air was filled with the stench of corruption, and the very earth seemed to tremble with the power of the Shadow.

Rachel knew this was their last chance. If they failed here, all of Eldoria would be lost. Taking a deep breath, she drew her sword and led her companions into battle.

The battle was long and hard, but in the end Rachel and her friends won. The Shadow was destroyed, its darkness banished from Eldoria. After the artifact was destroyed, the corrupted creatures were restored to their former selves and the land began to heal.

Rachel and her companions were hailed as heroes, the saviors of Eldoria. But even though the battle was won, Rachel knew their work wasn't done. The shadow was a symptom of a deeper problem, a darkness that still lingered in the hearts of some.

Rachel vowed to continue her fight for peace and justice to ensure Eldoria would never again be threatened by darkness. And so, with her companions by her side, she embarked on a new journey that will take her to even greater heights and even deeper challenges.

CHAPTER TWO

The City of Lumina

The euphoria of victory was short-lived. Even though the Shadowmaker was gone, whispers of concern lingered. Rumors spoke of ancient threats resurfacing, shadows flickering in the forgotten corners of Eldoria. Determined to understand this new danger, Rachel and her companions head to a city shrouded in mystery: Lumina.

Their journey led them through a breathtaking landscape painted by the caress of the sun on snow-capped peaks and pulsating valleys. Blackberry, always grumpy, complained about the lack of mushrooms along the way, while Kael regaled them with stories of brave elven battles. Lumina, ever gentle, hummed soothing tunes that calmed the air and kept hope alive.

Finally, a view beyond imagination opened up on the clouds penetrating the mountain range. In the sky floated floating islands adorned with crystals that shone like captured stars. They were connected by bridges of pure light, creating a dazzling cityscape unlike anything Rachel had ever seen. This was Lumina, the city of dreams.

As they stepped onto the beam of light, they were greeted warmly by the Luminarians, beings created from pure energy and shimmering with inner light. Their leader, a hypnotizing glow named Solaris, greeted Rachel with a knowing smile. He explained that Eldoria was not just a physical realm, but a tapestry woven from dreams and imaginations. Even as the Shadowshard was destroyed, it awakened a deeper darkness that threatened to dissolve the very fabric of their world.

Rachel learns that she's not just an outsider, but a "dreamspawn" whose connection to reality could bridge the gaps in Eldoria's waning magic. The long-lost secrets he was meant to uncover resided in the city itself, hidden in the dreamscape, waiting to be unlocked.

Days turned into weeks as Rachel delved into the city's mysterious libraries, guided by learned luminaries. In dreamscapes, she battled monstrous nightmares, unraveled mysterious riddles whispered by ancient echoes, and pieced together fragments of a forgotten past. She discovers that Eldoria was once divided and its magic broken by a cataclysmic event. The shadow was only a symptom, a fragment of darkness that now threatened to tear the realm apart again.

The deeper she went, the more Rachel questioned her own identity. Were these memories really hers, or echoes of Dreamweaver who had come before? Each revelation blurred the lines between reality and dreamland, leaving her teetering on the edge of something profound.

But amid the confusion, one truth remained clear: the fate of Eldoria rested on her shoulders. Driven by unwavering determination and a newfound sense of purpose, Rachel made a vow. He uncovers the secrets of Lumina, mends the broken magic of Eldoria, and faces the darkness head on.

And so began another chapter in which Rachel, Dreamweaver, stepped into the heart of the unknown to light the way ahead.

The load of prophecy settled heavily on Rachel. Unraveling the metropolis's secrets and techniques felt like chasing shadows, each revelation leading to some other unanswered question. She dreamt of forgotten battles, whispered of with reverence through the Luminarians, however the reminiscences felt hazy, incomplete. The most effective steady become the growing unease inside the town, a palpable tremor in the dreamscape because the encroaching darkness neared.

One twilight, Lumina pulsed with an eerie glow. Solaris, his normally serene face etched with fear, introduced that the darkness had discovered a key: a corrupted Dreamweaver, twisted by means of the equal historical force that shattered Eldoria. This rogue weaver changed into manipulating their collective dreams, sowing discord and worry, weakening the world from inside.

The council proposed a daring plan: input the corrupted dreamscape, confront the rogue weaver, and sever their connection to the darkness. but, coming into a corrupted dream turned into similar to walking into a waking nightmare, fraught with unpredictable risks and potentially irreversible consequences.

no matter the risks, Rachel, fueled via a fierce dedication and a developing information of her own unique powers, volunteered. Solaris located a shimmering pendant around her neck, imbuing it with the combined magic of Lumina. "this will anchor you to fact," he explained, "a lifeline if you are lost inside the chaos."

Bidding farewell to her partners, Rachel plunged into the depths of the corrupted dreamscape. The once ethereal metropolis warped right into a grotesque mockery of itself, homes crumbling and shadows writhing with malice. mammoth figures, figments of nightmares given shape, lunged at her, fueled by the weaver's dark affect.

the use of her newfound Dreamweaver capabilities, Rachel weaved illusions to distract the creatures, her thoughts growing weary with every passing second. The pendant pulsed, a comforting reminder of her venture. eventually, she reached the heart of the dreamscape, a desolate desolate tract dominated via a towering, shadowy determine.

The rogue weaver, their shape shrouded in darkness, identified Rachel with a chilling snarl. They engaged in a fierce battle, weaving nightmares towards dreams, light against shadow. The pendant hummed, caution her of her dwindling electricity.

In a desperate gambit, Rachel drew upon the reminiscences of beyond Dreamweavers, channeling their collective expertise and wish. The dreamscape shimmered, the darkness momentarily receding. She saw a glimpse of the weaver's past, a flicker of pain and betrayal that twisted their coronary heart.

the use of this newfound expertise, Rachel presented no longer a combat, but empathy. She stated the shared ache, the shared preference for peace. The weaver faltered, the darkness around them flickering.

all at once, Solaris' voice boomed through the dreamscape, guiding Rachel closer to a hidden supply of pure magic inside the corrupted weaver. Channeling it, she severed their connection to the darkness, now not with pressure, however with information and a spark of shared light.

The dreamscape shattered, transporting Rachel back to Lumina. Exhausted however positive, she discovered herself surrounded by means of cheers and relieved faces. The rogue weaver, now free from the darkness, awaited, their eyes brimming with gratitude.

The victory, but, felt bittersweet. Rachel knew this become simply the beginning. The source of the encroaching darkness remained, and its tendrils still stretched in the direction of Eldoria. but for now, a delicate peace settled over the metropolis of dreams, and Rachel, the Dreamweaver, emerged as a image of desire, prepared to stand the subsequent project, armed with newfound abilties and the growing know-how of her specific position on this fantastical realm.

Upon arrival in Lumina, Rachel gasped. Floating islands, decorated with crystals that shimmered like captured stars, soared above the clouds, connected by means of bridges of natural mild. The

Luminarians, beings of natural power and shimmering smiles, welcomed her with warm temperature that radiated like sunshine.

Their chief, Solaris, his form aglow with celestial light, explained that Eldoria wasn't only a realm, however a tapestry woven from dreams and creativeness. The Shadowshard, though destroyed, had woke up a deeper darkness, one which threatened to get to the bottom of the very fabric of their global. And Rachel, selected through fate, was extra than simply an interloper; she become a Dreamweaver, one whose connection to fact ought to bridge the gaps in Eldoria's fading magic.

The long-misplaced secrets and techniques she was to discover resided within the metropolis itself, hidden in the dreamscape, ready to be unlocked. the weight of prophecy settled on Rachel's shoulders. Solaris observed historic battles, whispered of with reverence, but the reminiscences felt hazy, incomplete.

decided, she delved into the city's libraries, guided with the aid of scholarly Luminarians. Lumina, ever mild, hummed calming melodies even as Bramble, ever the grump, grumbled about lacking mushrooms. Kael, but, thrived within the airy town, his Elven spirit resonating with the magic pulsing below its streets.

Nights unfolded inside the Dreamscape, a realm in which reality bent to its personal guidelines. Rachel battled large nightmares, each victory revealing fragments of a forgotten past. She observed that Eldoria become fractured, its magic broken by a cataclysmic event - the identical pressure that birthed the Shadowshard.

One dream discovered a chilling reality: the supply of the encroaching darkness wasn't simply an entity, however a distorted echo of herself - a rogue Dreamweaver corrupted by using the same historical pressure. This darkish mirror of Rachel manipulated their collective goals, sowing discord and worry, weakening the area from inside.

The council proposed a risky direction: enter the corrupted dreamscape, confront the rogue weaver, and sever their connection to the darkness. This supposed venturing right into a waking nightmare, fraught with unpredictable dangers and potentially irreversible results.

driven with the aid of her developing knowledge of her own unique powers and a fierce need to guard Eldoria, Rachel volunteered. Solaris positioned a shimmering pendant around her neck, imbuing it with the blended magic of Lumina. "this may anchor you to truth," he warned, "a lifeline if you are misplaced in the chaos."

Bidding farewell to her companions, Rachel plunged into the corrupted dreamscape. The once airy town warped into a gruesome mockery of itself, homes crumbling and shadows writhing with malice. giant figures, figments of nightmares given shape, lunged at her, fueled by using the weaver's darkish influence.

With every passing second, fatigue gnawed at her, but the pendant pulsed, a comforting reminder of her project. finally, she reached the coronary heart of the dreamscape, a desolate wasteland ruled by using a shadowy determine - the rogue weaver.

Their battle raged, weaving nightmares against desires, light in opposition to shadow. but as Rachel fought, she noticed beyond the darkness, glimpses of the weaver's past, a flicker of pain and betrayal that twisted their heart.

rather than wielding brute force, Rachel channeled empathy, imparting expertise and a shared spark of wish. The dreamscape shimmered, the darkness momentarily receding. The rogue weaver faltered, their eyes full of confusion.

collectively, they severed the connection to the darkness, no longer with violence, however with compassion. The dreamscape shattered, transporting them lower back to Lumina. although exhausted, Rachel knew this was simply the start. The authentic mastermind in the back of the darkness remained, and its tendrils still stretched towards Eldoria.

but for now, a delicate peace settled over the town of goals. Rachel, the Dreamweaver, emerged more potent, no longer only a hero, but a beacon of desire, prepared to face the subsequent undertaking, armed with newfound capabilities and a developing understanding of herself and the magical realm she now referred to as domestic.

CHAPTER THREE

The Prophecy Unveiled

News of Rachel's victory over the rogue Dreamweaver resonated all through Eldoria just like the chimes of a celestial bell. but, the birthday party turned into laced with an undercurrent of unease. The source of the darkness remained veiled, its tendrils still accomplishing in the direction of the coronary heart of the realm.

pushed by means of a burning desire to understand and quell the looming hazard, Rachel plunged deeper into the mysteries of Lumina. Guided by Solaris and the smart Luminarians, she delved into ancient libraries, their partitions buzzing with whispers of forgotten lore. amongst weathered scrolls and glowing tablets, she stumbled upon a hidden chamber pulsating with airy electricity.

There, etched on a mural made from stardust, lay the Prophecy of Eldoria. Verses of shimmering light whispered of a time while mild and darkness waged struggle, fracturing the realm and shattering its magic. They foretold the rise of a "Mystic Seeker," one born from a international past, destined to fix the fractures and restore stability.

As Rachel traced the symbols with trembling hands, Solaris confirmed her suspicions: she turned into the Mystic Seeker. The prophecy echoed the goals that had haunted her considering that arriving in Eldoria, fragments of a future she was slowly piecing together.

triumph over with awe and trepidation, Rachel devoured the prophecy's cryptic verses. It talked about hidden trials, mythical allies, and treacherous landscapes that confounded the laws of nature. each step in her journey, from confronting the Shadowshard to fighting the rogue weaver, were prophesied, yet the course beforehand remained shrouded in ambiguity.

Her preliminary fear became eclipsed by way of a fierce willpower. This turned into extra than only a responsibility; it turned into a calling that resonated deep inside her soul. Lumina, her voice laced with unwavering notion, reassured her. "The prophecy is but a manual, young Dreamweaver. Your real electricity lies for your unwavering spirit and the connections you forge along the way."

therefore began Rachel's odyssey in earnest. Following the whispers of the prophecy, she ventured past the floating islands of Lumina. She traversed whispering forests guarded by using historical treants, their bark etched with secrets of the ages. She navigated solar-scorched deserts wherein sphinxes posed riddles guarded by sizzling winds. each come upon tested her braveness and resourcefulness, forging alliances with enigmatic creatures and unlocking dormant powers inside herself.

within the twilight realm of the Feywild, she befriended a mischievous Sprite named Willow, whose playful pranks masked a deep properly of understanding. within the depths of the Crystal Caverns, she earned the honor of a stoic Dwarven King, his coronary heart softened by way of her actual spirit. With each ally, Rachel's knowledge of Eldoria deepened, unveiling the problematic tapestry of its records and magic.

The prophecy additionally warned of bold foes who would are looking for to obstruct her progress. inside the shadowed valleys of the Gloomhollow, she faced wraiths fueled by historic grudges, their contact draining no longer just life, however memories. within the smoldering ruins of a fallen country, she faced a cunning sorceress, her strength fueled by stolen magic and a thirst for dominion.

thru each struggle, Rachel honed her abilities, weaving goals and manipulating reality with growing finesse. The pendant proficient by using Solaris pulsed with renewed brilliance, a testomony to her growing connection to Eldoria's magic.

but, as victories piled up, a nagging question lingered: who turned into the mastermind at the back of the encroaching darkness? the solution, the prophecy warned, lay hidden in the Echoing Ruins, a forgotten city whispered to preserve the important thing to Eldoria's past and the actual face of her enemy.

With a resolute heart and a band of unswerving companions by means of her side, Rachel set sail towards the Echoing Ruins, ready to stand her best assignment but and unveil the truth that would shape the destiny of Eldoria.

The voyage to the Echoing Ruins become fraught with peril. tremendous sea serpents with eyes like molten lava rose from the depths, their scales impervious to traditional weapons. Will-o'-the-wisps, their airy flames covering wicked intent, led ships off track into treacherous shoals. but Rachel and her companions, every wielding their unique competencies, braved the dangers, fuelled with the aid of the know-how that within the Echoing Ruins lay the important thing to the genuine enemy and the prophecy's achievement.

finally, because the sun dipped under the horizon, casting lengthy shadows throughout the waves, they saw it: a metropolis growing from the ocean, its once majestic towers now crumbling husks, their surfaces etched with swirling glyphs that appeared to writhe inside the fading mild. This changed into the Echoing Ruins, a desolate monument to an extended-forgotten tragedy.

As they navigated the town's treacherous streets, the chilling silence became damaged simplest with the aid of the echoes in their own footsteps and the whispering wind. homes leaned precariously, threatening to fall apart underneath the burden of centuries. bizarre, otherworldly energies crackled within the air, sending shivers down their spines.

Their seek led them to a relevant plaza, ruled by means of a monolithic structure embellished with intricate carvings depicting scenes of both concord and devastation. It became right here, in step with the prophecy, that the fact could be found out.

As Rachel located her hand on the bloodless stone, a wave of strength pulsed through her, transporting her right into a kaleidoscope of recollections. She saw Eldoria in its high, a realm of vibrant lifestyles and magic. Then, darkness descended, twisted via an entity cloaked in shadows, its motives shrouded in malice. the world fractured, magic shattered, and the Echoing Ruins were born as a testament to the tragedy.

The imaginative and prescient ended abruptly, leaving Rachel gasping for breath, the burden of records heavy on her shoulders. Now she understood - the supply of the darkness wasn't just an entity, however the embodiment of an ancient grudge, a fraction of Eldoria's shattered magic twisted through hate. It turned into part of Eldoria itself, looking for to devour the whole.

all at once, a chilling laughter echoed through the plaza. A discern materialized from the shadows, its shape swirling with darkish energy - the embodiment of the prophecy's cryptic warnings. It called itself the Shadowborn, the fractured half of Eldoria's coronary heart, and it aimed to say the entire, erasing the light and plunging the realm into eternal darkness.

This wasn't a war of blades and spells, Rachel realized. It turned into a warfare for the very soul of Eldoria. She regarded to her companions, their faces grim but resolute. each held a fragment of the solution, a chunk of the magic had to heal the fractured realm.

Willow, the Sprite, danced, weaving illusions that careworn and distracted the Shadowborn. Kael, the Elven warrior, fought with the grace of a whirlwind, deflecting its darkish power blasts. Bramble, the grumpy Gnome, channeled the earth's magic, raising stone partitions to obstruct its increase.

And Rachel, the Mystic Seeker, drew upon the energy of dreams and recollections. She wove tales of Eldoria's past, of the unity and love that after bound the area collectively. each reminiscence, each whispered tale, chipped away at the Shadowborn's darkness, reminding it of what it as soon as became, of the connection it nevertheless shared with the entire.

The conflict raged, the plaza echoing with the conflict of mild and shadow. simply as their strength waned, Rachel had an epiphany. The prophecy by no means mentioned destroying the Shadowborn, but of recuperation it. With a surge of willpower, she reached out, no longer with weapons however with empathy.

She shared the recollections of Eldoria's splendor, of the love and joy that existed inside its various beings. The Shadowborn faltered, its form flickering as if stuck between two currents. Tears, now not of malice however of ache, streamed down its shadowy face.

In that second, Rachel understood. The Shadowborn wasn't the enemy, but a lost a part of Eldoria yearning to be whole once more. With a very last push of compassion, she supplied a easy message: "You are not alone. you're a part of us."

as though a dam had broken, the Shadowborn's darkness dissipated, merging with the mild emanating from Rachel and her partners. The fragmented magic of Eldoria started to mend, sewing together the injuries of the beyond.

The Echoing Ruins pulsed with renewed electricity, not a symbol of tragedy however of wish. The sky above, as soon as shrouded in gloom, cleared, revealing a celebrity-studded expanse. The battle became gained, now not by using destruction, however by knowledge and recognition.

however Rachel knew their journey became some distance from over. The scars of the beyond wouldn't heal in a single day. There could be more to do, more darkness to confront, each inside and without

CHAPTER FOUR

The Trials of Elemental Harmony

With the shadow of the Echoing Ruins receding and a delicate peace settling over Eldoria, a newfound willpower simmered inside Rachel. The prophecy may were partly fulfilled, but her role as the Mystic Seeker changed into some distance from over. To grow to be the proper embodiment of the prophecy, she had to show herself worth, no longer just via acts of valor, but by way of forging a deeper reference to the very essence of Eldoria: its elemental coronary heart.

Guided through whispers at the wind and shimmering luminescence emanating from the earth, Rachel observed herself drawn to a hidden grove, its historic timber pulsating with an otherworldly power. here, within the heart of the Whispering Woods, she met the enigmatic Sylvani, their voices like rustling leaves and their eyes sparkling with the brilliance of fireflies. They talked about the pains of Elemental harmony, historic assessments designed to assess the worthiness of the Mystic Seeker, a gauntlet that would push Rachel to her limits and free up powers dormant within her.

With a resolute coronary heart, Rachel widespread the project. The Sylvani defined that every trial would be overseen through a effective spirit – Ignis, the fiery lord of the forge; Aquaria, the serene mistress of the deep; Zephyr, the swift and playful master of the winds; and Gaia, the stoic and smart mother of the earth. each spirit represented a essential component of Eldoria's magic, and each trial might test a one of a kind facet of Rachel's individual.

First, Ignis awaited her in the depths of a volcanic cavern, its air thick with heat and the clang of unseen hammers. There, Rachel faced a trial of strength of will, forced to forge a weapon no longer with brute strength, however with the managed consciousness of her spirit. Guided with the aid of Ignis's fiery pronouncements, she tempered her will, gaining knowledge of to channel her feelings into targeted bursts of innovative strength, in the end forging a shimmering blade of pure light.

rising from the volcano, invigorated and empowered, Rachel located herself amidst swirling winds atop a treacherous mountain height. Zephyr, his voice carried at the gusts, challenged her agility and wit. She navigated treacherous ledges, solved riddles whispered on the wind, and danced with the currents, honing her reflexes and instinct till she moved with the grace of a hovering fowl.

The tranquil depths of a hidden lake led Rachel to Aquaria, her shape shimmering like moonlight on water. here, the trial become one of compassion and understanding. Rachel delved into the lake's depths, encountering creatures of fantasy and legend, every harassed with the aid of their own sorrows. via being attentive to their stories and imparting empathy, she calmed their bothered spirits, gaining knowledge of the electricity of connection and the language of the coronary heart.

sooner or later, under the historic roots of the Whispering Woods, Rachel met Gaia, her voice as deep and constant as the thrashing of the earth's heart. The very last trial examined her remedy and connection to the herbal global. She navigated labyrinthine roots, nurtured ill vegetation together with her newfound power, and learned to talk the language of the earth, forging a deep bond with the very basis of Eldoria.

With each triumph, Rachel felt a surge of electricity flow via her, her connection to the factors deepening. She was no longer simply the Mystic Seeker, but a conduit, channeling the uncooked magic of Eldoria itself. Now, armed with newfound skills, cast alliances with the fundamental guardians, and a coronary heart brimming with know-how and compassion, Rachel stood equipped for whatever challenges awaited her at the path closer to fulfilling the prophecy and ensuring the real harmony of Eldoria.

The echoes of the trials resonated within Rachel, leaving an indelible mark on her soul. every undertaking had now not most effective honed her capabilities but also found out a profound truth approximately herself and the interconnectedness of Eldoria's elements. but, the whispers on the wind carried news of a developing unease. The shadow of the Echoing Ruins hadn't absolutely dissipated. Unease grew among the Feywild creatures, and whispers stated corrupted beings stirring in forgotten corners of the world.

Guided by using her deepening connection to the factors, Rachel set out to research. Zephyr led her on soaring currents, revealing patches of darkened forests in which as soon as thriving lifestyles had wilted. Aquaria unveiled polluted waterways wherein once pristine existence struggled. Ignis whispered testimonies of volcanic eruptions emanating from unnaturally active areas. Gaia's deep rumble mentioned tremors annoying the non violent shut eye of the earth.

The signs have been undeniable: a malevolent force, emboldened by the shadow's weakening, aimed to disrupt the delicate balance of Eldoria's elements, plunging the realm into chaos. the pains had prepared Rachel, but the true take a look at was yet to come back.

becoming a member of forces together with her elemental allies, Rachel devised a plan. They might strike on the heart of the corruption, severing its tendrils from each detail in flip. the journey would be fraught with danger, each element presenting its very own specific demanding situations.

inside the sizzling deserts, fueled by using Ignis's fiery spirit, Rachel confronted tremendous creatures born from molten rock, their hides impervious to conventional guns. She discovered to channel the wilderness's harsh beauty, wielding warmth waves and sandstorms to her advantage.

inside the coronary heart of the swirling Mistwood, guided through Zephyr's playful whispers, Rachel confronted illusions and treacherous loos conjured by means of the corrupting pressure. She honed her agility and short questioning, dodging spectral assaults and using the wind's electricity to navigate the moving panorama.

under the murky depths of corrupted waterways, Aquaria's serene guidance shone through. Rachel encountered colossal leviathans and poisonous waters, gaining knowledge of to communicate with the once non violent denizens of the deep, turning their fury towards the corruption.

in the quaking coronary heart of the earth, Gaia's stoic expertise proved valuable. Rachel navigated collapsing caverns and battled mutated rock creatures, drawing on this planet's strength to fix the wounded land and sever the corruption's maintain.

With every victory, Rachel grew more potent, her connection to the elements deepening. She become no longer just a conduit, but a weaver, manipulating the uncooked magic of Eldoria with newfound grace and motive. but, she knew the ultimate war of words awaited.

Deep inside a forbidden canyon, pulsating with a malevolent strength, resided the source of the corruption. It changed into a being of natural discord, fueled by way of the remnants of the Shadowborn's fractured essence. It sought to tear the factors apart, plunging Eldoria into an everlasting conflict of nature.

The final warfare raged, a conflict of elements and wills. Rachel, drawing upon the lessons found out and the strength of her allies, danced through the typhoon. She wove shields of fire and wind, wielded the earth's electricity, and commanded the waft of water, all orchestrated with an unwavering spirit.

in the end, it wasn't just brute force that won the day, but understanding. Rachel, channeling the collective will of Eldoria's factors, reached out to the center of the corrupted being, imparting now not destruction however empathy and the promise of recovery. The darkness flickered, its hold loosening.

With a very last surge of purified power, Rachel severed the last tendrils of corruption. The being dissolved, leaving in the back of a sigh of comfort that echoed thru the canyon. Peace settled over the land, the elements aligning yet again in a harmonious dance.

Rachel had emerged positive, not just because the Mystic Seeker, but as a symbol of team spirit and balance. but, she knew the adventure wasn't over. The scars of the corruption could heal, but the training discovered might all the time guide her as she persevered to shield the concord of Eldoria, all the time certain to the magic that flowed through its veins.

CHAPTER FIVE

Shadows of Discord

The echoes of the rigors resonated inside Rachel, leaving an indelible mark on her soul. every task had not only honed her abilties however also found out a profound fact about herself and the interconnectedness of Eldoria's factors. but, the whispers on the wind carried news of a growing unease. The shadow of the Echoing Ruins hadn't completely dissipated. Unease grew among the Feywild creatures, and whispers spoke of corrupted beings stirring in forgotten corners of the realm.

Guided by means of her deepening connection to the factors, Rachel set out to analyze. Zephyr led her on hovering currents, revealing patches of darkened forests in which as soon as thriving life had wilted. Aquaria unveiled polluted waterways where once pristine lifestyles struggled. Ignis whispered tales of volcanic eruptions emanating from unnaturally active regions. Gaia's deep rumble stated tremors disturbing the non violent shut eye of the earth.

The signs had been plain: a malevolent pressure, emboldened by the shadow's weakening, aimed to disrupt the sensitive stability of Eldoria's elements, plunging the area into chaos. the trials had prepared Rachel, however the real take a look at was but to come.

joining forces together with her elemental allies, Rachel devised a plan. They could strike at the heart of the corruption, severing its tendrils from each element in turn. the adventure might be fraught with threat, each element providing its own unique demanding situations.

within the sizzling deserts, fueled by using Ignis's fiery spirit, Rachel confronted significant creatures born from molten rock, their hides impervious to conventional guns. She learned to channel the wilderness's harsh beauty, wielding warmth waves and sandstorms to her gain.

within the heart of the swirling Mistwood, guided by way of Zephyr's playful whispers, Rachel confronted illusions and treacherous bogs conjured with the aid of the corrupting pressure. She honed her agility and quick thinking, dodging spectral attacks and the usage of the wind's electricity to navigate the transferring panorama.

underneath the murky depths of corrupted waterways, Aquaria's serene steerage shone thru. Rachel encountered mammoth leviathans and poisonous waters, learning to communicate with the as soon as peaceful denizens of the deep, turning their fury against the corruption.

inside the quaking coronary heart of the earth, Gaia's stoic awareness proved priceless. Rachel navigated collapsing caverns and battled mutated rock creatures, drawing on the planet's power to mend the wounded land and sever the corruption's keep.

With each victory, Rachel grew more potent, her connection to the elements deepening. She turned into not just a conduit, however a weaver, manipulating the raw magic of Eldoria with newfound grace and purpose. but, she knew the remaining war of words awaited.

Deep within a forbidden canyon, pulsating with a malevolent energy, resided the supply of the corruption. It become a being of natural discord, fueled via the remnants of the Shadowborn's fractured essence. It sought to tear the factors apart, plunging Eldoria into an everlasting warfare of nature.

The very last war raged, a clash of elements and wills. Rachel, drawing upon the lessons found out and the strength of her allies, danced through the storm. She wove shields of hearth and wind, wielded the earth's strength, and commanded the glide of water, all orchestrated with an unwavering spirit.

ultimately, it wasn't just brute force that gained the day, but expertise. Rachel, channeling the collective will of Eldoria's elements, reached out to the core of the corrupted being, offering now not destruction however empathy and the promise of healing. The darkness flickered, its keep loosening.

With a final surge of purified energy, Rachel severed the last tendrils of corruption. The being dissolved, leaving behind a sigh of comfort that echoed via the canyon. Peace settled over the land, the factors aligning yet again in a harmonious dance.

Rachel had emerged successful, no longer simply because the Mystic Seeker, however as a symbol of cohesion and stability. but, she knew the journey wasn't over. The scars of the corruption might heal, however the instructions found out could forever guide her as she persisted to shield the concord of Eldoria, forever certain to the magic that flowed via its veins.As Rachel endured her exploration of Eldoria's enigmatic secrets and techniques, the veil among dimensions grew thin, revealing the life of malevolent entities called the Shadows of Discord. those dark forces, pushed by way of an insatiable preference to get to the bottom of the very material of truth, posed a grave hazard to the delicate stability that held Eldoria collectively.

In her adventure, Rachel found the historical prophecies that foretold the coming of these malevolent beings. Whispers of drawing close chaos echoed thru the mystical landscapes, and Rachel understood the gravity of her quest. to face the Shadows of Discord, she wanted more than simply her own strength; she wanted allies who shared her determination to guard Eldoria.

United with a various institution of newfound companions, each owning specific skills and powers, Rachel launched into a dangerous mission to confront the Shadows of Discord. The camaraderie many of the group started to blossom, and the genuine electricity of harmony and friendship emerged as a beacon of wish inside the face of darkness.

the adventure via Eldoria changed into fraught with demanding situations, as the Shadows of Discord unleashed their sinister affect, distorting truth and plunging the once colourful landscapes into ominous shadows. Rachel and her allies faced trials that tested not only their individual strengths however also the electricity in their bond.

because the war between light and shadow intensified, the genuine nature of Eldoria's destiny spread out. The historical forces that ruled the area have been at the verge of a cosmic conflict, and the fate of the entire global hung within the balance. Rachel's determination, mixed with the unwavering aid of her allies, became the catalyst for a formidable counterforce against the encroaching darkness.

in the heart of Eldoria, amidst the swirling shadows and echoing discord, Rachel and her allies stood united, equipped to stand the remaining confrontation. The Shadows of Discord loomed menacingly, seeking to unravel the very essence of the world they inhabited. It was a struggle not only for survival, however for the renovation of Eldoria's harmony and the triumph of mild over the ever-encroaching shadows.

The battleground was set, and the clash between Rachel's group and the Shadows of Discord erupted in a spectacular display of magical prowess and ethereal chaos. Each member of the alliance unleashed their unique abilities, weaving together a tapestry of light and power to counter the malevolent forces that sought to tear Eldoria apart.

As the battle raged on, the true strength of unity became evident. Rachel's allies, once strangers, now fought side by side as a cohesive unit. Their combined efforts created a harmonious symphony of power that resonated through the very core of Eldoria, pushing back against the encroaching shadows.

However, the Shadows of Discord were relentless. Dark tendrils of energy snaked through the air, attempting to unravel the fabric of reality itself. The landscape warped and shifted, mirroring the tumultuous struggle between light and shadow. The fate of Eldoria teetered on the precipice, and the weight of responsibility pressed heavily on Rachel's shoulders.

In a pivotal moment, a surge of newfound strength coursed through Rachel. Unbeknownst to her, Eldoria responded to the unity and determination of its protectors. The ancient energies that permeated the realm intertwined with Rachel's own, granting her a profound connection to the very essence of the world she sought to save.

With a surge of inspiration, Rachel rallied her allies. "Together, we are the guardians of Eldoria! Let our unity be the light that banishes the shadows!" she declared, her words echoing through the battlefield.

Empowered by their shared purpose, Rachel and her allies intensified their efforts. The Shadows of Discord recoiled as the combined might of friendship and determination overwhelmed their malevolence. Light surged forth, dispelling the darkness and restoring Eldoria to its former glory.

As the last remnants of the Shadows of Discord dissipated, a newfound serenity settled over the realm. The once-distorted landscapes regained their vibrancy, and the ominous shadows were replaced by the warm embrace of light.

Eldoria, though scarred by the battle, had been saved from the brink of destruction. Rachel and her allies, now bound by a deep and unbreakable connection forged in the crucible of adversity, stood together as the saviors of their world.

The echoes of their triumph resonated through Eldoria, a testament to the indomitable power of unity and friendship in the face of discord. As the group looked towards the horizon, they knew that their journey was far from over. The mysteries of Eldoria still beckoned, and new adventures awaited them, united against any shadows that dared to threaten the harmony of their cherished realm.

CHAPTER SIX

The Timeless Sacrifice

As Rachel stood at the precipice of destiny, the weight of the arena pressed upon her shoulders. The fate of Eldoria hung inside the stability, and the swirling mists of uncertainty veiled the course in advance. The ominous forces of darkness, embodied in a malevolent presence called the Shadow King, threatened to devour everything she held dear.

The air crackled with anxiety as Rachel surveyed the battlefield, a panorama scarred by way of the relentless conflict between mild and shadow. Her partners, battered and bruised, regarded to her for guidance, their eyes reflecting a mix of worry and hope. Eldoria's remaining stand opened up in the dim glow of the waning sun, casting long shadows across the as soon as-stunning realm.

A voice, each haunting and seductive, whispered in Rachel's thoughts, tempting her with guarantees of electricity and an get away from the approaching doom. The charm of an less complicated route tugged at her solve, however deep inside her coronary heart, she knew that real heroes had been cast in the crucible of sacrifice.

With a heavy heart, Rachel took a step forward, her willpower unwavering. The ancient artifacts, pulsating with residual magic, surrounded her. every carried a chunk of Eldoria's essence, a connection to the very material of the area. the realization dawned upon her – to sever the Shadow King's grip on Eldoria, she needed to sacrifice a part of the realm's essence.

As Rachel made her desire, a surge of energy coursed via her veins. The artifacts spoke back to her sacrifice, unleashing a stunning mild that enveloped the battlefield. The Shadow King recoiled, his sinister laughter echoing through the chaos. however Rachel stood company, her sacrifice shielding her allies and pushing lower back the encroaching darkness.

In that timeless moment, Eldoria shifted. The very threads of its lifestyles rewove themselves, developing a tapestry where sacrifice and bravery intertwined. the realm started to heal, scars fading and nature reclaiming its lost splendor. The sacrifice had turn out to be a beacon, a symbol of hope that might resonate thru Eldoria's history.

as the echoes of the climactic war of words faded, Rachel stood amidst the renewed realm. The sacrifices made were not forgotten, etched into the annals of Eldoria's lore. a brand new chapter had began, one in which the undying sacrifice of a brave hero have become a guiding mild for generations to come back.

CHAPTER SEVEN

The Awakening

As the moon cast its silvery gaze upon the world, an impossible to resist tug echoed inside Rachel. The artifact, dormant considering she first arrived in Eldoria, pulsed with an otherworldly light, its name unmistakable. Guided through its airy glow, she retraced her steps, leaving at the back of the familiar consolation of Lumina and venturing returned into the heart of the Enchanted forest.

The as soon as vibrant route regarded unique now, shadows deeper, whispers carried at the rustling leaves greater pressing. memories flickered, not of her personal beyond, but of a forgotten time, a time while the artifact hummed with life, a gateway to any other global.

achieving the clearing in which the portal had first opened, she found the very air crackling with anticipation. The artifact throbbed in her hand, a beacon inside the deepening night. As she positioned it upon the historic sigil carved into the ground, the energy intensified, swirling around her in a dizzying vortex.

The earth hummed, the bushes swayed in unison, after which, with a blinding flash, the arena dissolved. whilst Rachel blinked her eyes open, she located herself standing in a foreign landscape. gone had been the airy crystal-studded islands and shimmering metropolis of Lumina. instead, she stood amidst towering redwoods, their historic branches shrouded in mist, the air thick with the fragrance of damp earth and pine needles.

Disoriented but undeterred, Rachel cautiously explored her environment. The air carried the faint echoes of unfamiliar languages, whispers of a colourful civilization lengthy faded. Ruins of large buildings, their structure not like something she'd visible in Eldoria, peeked through the dense foliage. This became no normal wooded area, but a lost international, awoke by using the artifact's call.

abruptly, a rustling sound within the undergrowth despatched shivers down her spine. emerging from the shadows turned into a creature in contrast to any she'd encountered earlier than – humanoid, yet cloaked in emerald leaves, its eyes glowing with an inner light. fear warred with curiosity in Rachel's heart. Who were those beings? What secrets did this sound asleep world preserve?

As she opened her mouth to talk, the creature knelt before her, its voice resonating with the melody of the woodland itself. "Welcome, selected one," it spoke, its phrases echoing in the historic language Rachel by some means understood. "we have awaited your arrival. The artifact has delivered you here, to fix the broken bridge among our worlds."

Rachel's jaw dropped. Mend a broken bridge? What did it mean? became she by hook or by crook liable for the fate of this forgotten civilization? Uncertainty churned within her, however the creature's mild demeanor and the yearning in its eyes sparked a flicker of wish.

Taking a deep breath, Rachel regularly occurring the burden of the unknown. "I don't know what i'm presupposed to do," she admitted, "but i'm here to concentrate. inform me your tale, tell me approximately your international."

And so, underneath the ancient redwoods, a new bankruptcy commenced. The story of a misplaced civilization, of a broken connection, and of a chance come upon that would rewrite the fate of worlds. As Rachel delved deeper into this hidden realm, she could discover a fact that would project the whole lot she concept she knew approximately herself and Eldoria, a fact that could for all time regulate the direction of her destiny.

CHAPTER EIGHT

Harmonizing Realms

The revelation within the lost world struck Rachel like a bolt of lightning. The artifact, the portal, her arrival — they were not random occurrences. She wasn't just the Mystic Seeker of Eldoria, however a bridge, a connection prophesied among nation-states.

Returning to Lumina, her coronary heart ablaze with newfound reason, Rachel sought the hidden library, its dusty cabinets whispering secrets and techniques waiting to be unearthed. Guided through Solaris and fueled by an urgent thirst for understanding, she delved into forgotten texts, their pages brittle with age and their script dwindled but amazing.

amongst forgotten myths and diminished maps, she stumbled upon a scroll, its floor shimmering with an otherworldly light. As she unfurled it, the script got here alive, coalescing into a imaginative and prescient – a tapestry woven from the threads of two worlds.

An image of Eldoria, vibrant and entire, reflected every other realm, lush and verdant, but shrouded in shadow. A shimmering bridge related them, pulsating with strength, however fractured, emitting cracks that spewed darkness. Then, figures appeared – a luminous Eldorian and a cloaked being from the other realm, their fingers outstretched in a plea for harmony.

The imaginative and prescient shifted, showing the fracturing of the bridge, a cataclysmic occasion as a result of greed and misunderstanding. Darkness spread, engulfing the alternative realm, while Eldoria become shielded however scarred. Then, amidst the chaos, a single discern emerged – a beacon of hope, radiating both the mild of Eldoria and the emerald glow of the misplaced global.

The scroll pulsed, the words forming themselves definitely: "whilst worlds fall, and shadows upward thrust, a Mystic Seeker, of nation-states born, shall mend the bridge, and balance repair."

Tears welled in Rachel's eyes. The prophecy reflected her very own story, her connection to the enchanted realm, and the calling she felt to heal both worlds. Now, the stakes have been clean – not simply the destiny of Eldoria, however the destiny of two civilizations trusted her moves.

Sharing the prophecy with her partners, a fireplace of solve ignited inside them. Kael, whose Elven ancestry whispered of historical alliances, talked about forging bonds with the misplaced realm. Bramble, his practical thoughts buzzing, strategized methods to repair the fractured bridge. Lumina, ever calm and smart, offered steering and solace, reminding them that empathy and information would be key.

thus commenced a brand new chapter in their journey. Guided by using the prophecy and fueled with the aid of a newfound motive, they launched into a quest to gather fragments of the bridge, scattered throughout each worlds. every fragment held a tale, a memory, a bit of the relationship misplaced. They confronted treacherous guardians, untangled historical riddles, and forged alliances with wary inhabitants of the enchanted realm.

As they collected the fragments, Rachel's expertise of the 2 worlds deepened. The darkness that plagued the opposite realm wasn't just an external chance, but a twisted echo of their own fear and mistrust. restoration one meant recovery the opposite, a delicate dance of bridging now not simply realms but hearts.

finally, with all of the fragments gathered, they stood earlier than the shattered bridge, its electricity resonating with their blended motive. Rachel, channeling the electricity of each worlds, wove the fragments collectively, now not just with magic, but with compassion and shared hope.

Slowly, the bridge shimmered, mending itself piece through piece. daylight streamed thru the repaired cracks, bathing the as soon as-shadowed realm in warm temperature. because the final connection changed into made, a wave of strength surged, erasing the darkness and restoring the bridge to its former glory.

standing at the crossroads of two worlds, Rachel took a deep breath. the journey were exhausting, however the genuine take a look at became yet to come back. The bridge was rebuilt, but the hearts of its human beings still wished restoration. as the Mystic Seeker, her position had advanced. She become not only a conduit of magic, however an ambassador, a image of harmony, destined to forge an enduring peace between two geographical regions forever certain through her exquisite presence.

Empowered by way of the revelation of her dual future and armed with the repaired bridge, Rachel stood prepared to stand the Shadows of Discord yet again. This time, her reason transcended mere protection. She wasn't simply the Mystic Seeker of Eldoria, but the embodiment of the harmonized realms, wielding the mixed magic of worlds.

The Shadows, emboldened via their previous encounter, unleashed a surge of darkness, engulfing Eldoria in a chilling twilight. Their whispers, amplified by way of the fractured bridge, sowed discord and worry amongst the Luminarians. but, Rachel stood firm, her eyes blazing with newfound solve.

She reached out together with her senses, not just into the cloth of Eldoria, however across the bridge, feeling the colourful energies of her own fact hum in reaction. It was a symphony of light and shadow, chaos and order, and inside it, she sought the concord that would vanquish the darkness.

With a flick of her wrist, she drew Eldoria's shimmering strength, weaving it right into a shield that deflected the Shadows' attacks. She countered their discord with melodies of her personal reality, vibrant chords that resonated with the essence of lifestyles and introduction.

Kael, inspired by means of the harmonized magic, danced thru the battlefield, his Elven grace infused with the agility of an historical warrior. Bramble, channeling the earth's power from both nation-states, raised partitions of emerald stone to impede the Shadows' strengthen. Lumina, her airy shape shimmering brighter than ever, soothed the frightened Luminarians, their desire rekindled by means of her calming presence.

The Shadows, amazed by this unified the front, recoiled momentarily. however their leader, a being of swirling darkness, rallied them, its voice booming with malice. "Your efforts are futile! One realm or two, darkness shall succeed!"

Undeterred, Rachel surged ahead, a beacon of harmonized light. She wove now not just spells, but know-how, bridging the space among the shadows and the mild within each being. She showed them the splendor of the interconnected worlds, the ability for peace and mutual increase.

The Shadows faltered, their bureaucracy flickering as the discord within them resonated with Rachel's message. one by one, they started to dissolve, drawn towards the mild, their darkness replaced by using whispers of remorse and craving for connection.

eventually, only the leader remained, its shape writhing in a desperate struggle. however even it couldn't face up to the pull of harmonized magic. Slowly, its darkness dissipated, revealing a weary spirit, its essence fractured with the aid of millennia of isolation and worry.

Rachel reached out, presenting now not judgment, however compassion. "You are not by myself," she said, her voice resonating with empathy. "we can forge a new course, one built on understanding and shared mild."

In that second, the very last Shadow dissolved, leaving behind a flicker of wish. The darkness that had plagued Eldoria receded, replaced with the aid of a gentle, harmonized glow. The bridge among the nation-states hummed with newfound balance, a testomony to the strength of cohesion and the Mystic Seeker who had bridged the gap.

The victory brought cheers and celebrations for the duration of Eldoria and past. however Rachel knew their work wasn't over. The scars of past discord would take time to heal, and the bridge required steady care. but, she faced the destiny with optimism, her heart brimming with the harmonized magic of worlds. She become not simply the Mystic Seeker, however a symbol of wish, a weaver of light, all the time sure to the destiny of two nation-states she had united.

because the celebrations in Lumina faded and the ultimate echoes of cheers dwindled, a quiet settled over Rachel. the load of obligation, although tempered by alleviation, lingered heavy on her shoulders. The Shadows of Discord is probably subdued, however the proper venture − recovery the fractured realms and forging lasting peace − had simply began.

information of the harmonized magic travelled rapidly, stirring interest and unease in same measure. Whispers reached Rachel of other geographical regions, hidden dimensions craving for connection, but cautious of Eldoria's newfound power. a few saw them as potential allies, others as threats desiring to be contained.

The bridge itself pulsed with a nascent sentience, mirroring the emotions coursing thru the connected geographical regions. At times, it shimmered with colourful energy, a testomony to the developing harmony. different instances, it flickered, reflecting the lingering distrust and fear.

pushed through an unwavering preference for understanding, Rachel launched into a sequence of diplomatic missions. She traversed the shimmering bridge, venturing into other realms each colourful and desolate. She encountered beings of pure light and creatures sculpted from living shadow, each with their personal history, fears, and goals.

With empathy as her weapon and the harmonized magic her bridge, Rachel facilitated dialogues, fostered cultural exchanges, and addressed long-held grievances. She became a weaver of narratives, sharing memories of both nation-states, highlighting their shared vulnerabilities and highlighting the potential for a brighter destiny.

but, there were folks who remained proof against trade. powerful entities, clinging to vintage prejudices and fearing the lack of their dominance, whispered insidious doubts and fuelled historical rivalries. They manipulated shadows, twisting fear into discord, and sought to sabotage the fragile peace Rachel had constructed.

Navigating this labyrinth of political intrigue and hidden agendas demanded greater than just magical prowess. Rachel needed to hone her know-how of human - or rather, interdimensional - emotions. She discovered to pick out subtle shifts in electricity, decipher hidden reasons, and navigate the murky waters of political maneuvering.

the journey wasn't without its setbacks. Alliances cast with painstaking attempt fractured underneath the sway of incorrect information. cunning manipulations led to misunderstandings and mistrust. Rachel herself confronted accusations of bias, stuck within the crossfire among competing hobbies.

yet, even amidst the darkness, glimmers of hope remained. Seeds of empathy planted for the duration of dialogues flourished, blossoming into acts of kindness and expertise. people, weary of conflict, defied their leaders' in pursuit of peace. Small but huge collaborations took root, fostering shared understanding and cultural exchange.

Rachel, fuelled by way of these glimmers of development, persisted. She organized grand gatherings throughout the bridge, inviting various representatives from all realms. through art, track, and shared storytelling, she fostered a feel of shared humanity, highlighting the beauty and power in their variations.

As accept as true with slowly blossomed, tentative agreements were formed. exchange routes were mounted, selling monetary interdependence and fostering mutual understanding. Joint studies initiatives tackled common threats, proving that collaboration should yield solutions past the attain of any single realm.

Years later, as Rachel stood staring at across the bridge, now a bustling hub of interdimensional cooperation, a feel of bittersweet satisfaction washed over her. the adventure had been exhausting, marked by means of moments of doubt and depression. yet, the as soon as fractured nation-states now hummed with the power of co-life, a testomony to the energy of empathy, information, and the unwavering notion in the possibility of peace.

though her function as the Mystic Seeker had advanced, her adventure turned into some distance from over. New challenges would stand up, disturbing her unique abilities and unwavering spirit.

but one component changed into certain: the bridge stood as a beacon of hope, a image of the solidarity Rachel had tirelessly strived for, a testament to the profound impact a single seeker, armed with empathy and courage, should have at the destiny of infinite worlds.

As time flowed and the interconnected nation-states flourished under the bridge's unifying hum, whispers of a distant, historic chance started to reach Rachel's ears. Legends talked about the Devourer, a cosmic entity of pure entropy, a being so ancient and substantial it existed earlier than advent itself, yearning to consume all existence and return it to the primordial void.

initial dismissals became to grave problem as fragmented visions flooded Rachel's mind. She saw galaxies collapse, entire dimensions gobbled, leaving behind only swirling tendrils of darkness. worry gripped the interconnected nation-states, their newfound solidarity threatened via the chilling prospect of cosmic oblivion.

understanding that going through the Devourer required not just collective might but a unified consciousness, Rachel launched into a monumental quest. She journeyed to the furthest corners of the interconnected realms, in search of historical information, forgotten lore, and whispers of beings effective enough to face towards such an entity.

Her quest led her to cryptic prophecies hidden inside death stars, to conversations with airy beings older than time, and to forgotten temples pulsating with the echoes of lost civilizations. Slowly, she pieced together the Devourer's origins and observed a chilling reality: the entity wasn't just a mindless force, however a being born from the collective fear and negativity of sentient lifestyles across the cosmos.

Armed with this understanding, Rachel knew an immediate assault would be futile. The Devourer thrived on fear, and any act of violence could simplest gasoline its strength. alternatively, she devised a daring plan: to counter its consuming darkness with a wave of positivity, a collective affirmation of existence, wish, and advent.

With the help of the interconnected nation-states, she initiated a assignment of exceptional scale. Artists from throughout dimensions collaborated on a surprising artwork, a tapestry woven from starlight and creativeness, showcasing the beauty and variety of existence. Musicians composed symphonies that resonated with the very cloth of truth, celebrating the joy of lifestyles in all its bureaucracy.

scholars and inventors pooled their knowledge, creating beacons that amplified and broadcast this message of hope across the vastness of area. As they worked, a wave of unprecedented team spirit swept thru the realms. old rivalries dwindled, changed through a collaborative spirit, a determination to face the Devourer collectively.

in the end, the culmination arrived. as the tapestry unfurled throughout the cosmic sky, its vibrant colours and problematic details painting a testament to the brilliance of advent, and because the symphony echoed via the void, carrying the collective song of lifestyles, Rachel felt a shift. The

Devourer, sensing the surge of positivity, faltered. Its tendrils recoiled, its eating darkness momentarily repelled.

In that moment of vulnerability, the combined might of the interconnected geographical regions unleashed a wave of pure creation. existence-giving electricity, fueled by way of wish and joy, poured forth, mending the cosmic wounds inflicted by using the Devourer, pushing lower back the tide of entropy.

Exhausted but successful, Rachel watched because the Devourer retreated, its shape shrinking back into the void. The chance wasn't eliminated, however for now, it had been contained. The interconnected realms, for all time modified by means of their shared struggle, had determined a brand new degree of harmony, a newfound appreciation for the delicate beauty of existence.

Rachel knew the Devourer may go back, its starvation for oblivion ever-present. however now, the realms had been organized. they had faced a cosmic danger collectively, forged bonds of agree with and cooperation, and determined the electricity of positivity inside the face of melancholy. This wasn't just a victory for Rachel, the Mystic Seeker, however for every being who dared to dream, to create, and to hope, a testament to the resilience of lifestyles and the boundless capacity of collaboration in the face of even the most ambitious foe.

And so, her adventure persisted, no longer just a lone seeker but a symbol of team spirit, a beacon of desire inside the good sized and ever-evolving tapestry of the interconnected geographical regions.

CHAPTER NINE

Everlasting Enchantment

The silence after the Devourer's retreat held a pregnant weight. comfort mingled with uncertainty. while the instant risk was vanquished, residual tremors echoed throughout the interconnected geographical regions. Fears lurked, whispering doubts approximately the Devourer's real defeat.

Rachel, sensing the unease, knew their harmony, solid in the face of oblivion, couldn't honestly deplete. It needed a reason, a shared vision beyond mere survival. therefore, she amassed representatives from across the nation-states, their numerous paperwork filling the grand corridor of Lumina.

Amidst whispers of reconstruction and lingering anxieties, Rachel proposed a daring imaginative and prescient: the Nexus venture. An ambitious project to map the full-size expanse of the interconnected geographical regions, uncovering misplaced civilizations, forgotten information, and hidden risks. It turned into a adventure of exploration, collaboration, and discovery, aimed toward forging a deeper know-how in their collective lifestyles.

The suggestion ignited a spark of wish. the prospect of venturing beyond familiar borders, of sharing knowledge and sources, resonated with the craving for team spirit. Alliances solidified, fueled with the aid of a shared desire to chart their future collectively.

hence began the Nexus task. Fleets of interdimensional ships, marvels of collaborative engineering, launched into expeditions. each carried various crews, their precise perspectives enriching the exploration. They charted celestial bodies, deciphered historic ruins, and encountered wondrous lifeforms, increasing their expertise of the cosmos and their region inside it.

the journey wasn't with out its challenges. unforeseen risks lurked in unexplored areas, checking out their harmony and resilience. ancient conflicts between long-forgotten civilizations resurfaced, threatening to fracture their newfound peace.

but inside each project, Rachel noticed an possibility. She fostered speak, reminding them in their shared warfare towards the Devourer. through international relations and empathy, she facilitated resolutions, showcasing the energy of collaboration over conflict.

because the Nexus challenge improved, they unearthed not just wonders but also forgotten mistakes, testaments to past civilizations fed on by way of greed and isolation. those discoveries served as stark reminders of the Devourer's ever-gift chance, urging them to stay vigilant and united.

Years later, Rachel, her hair now streaked with silver, stood overlooking a bustling galactic hub - Nexus metropolis, a testament to their collective adventure. various beings intermingled, sharing know-how, testimonies, and laughter. The interconnected realms, once disparate and frightened, now thrived in colourful concord.

yet, Rachel knew their work turned into a long way from over. The echoes of the Devourer nevertheless resonated, a reminder of the universe's delicate stability. but she faced the future with unwavering wish, her heart brimming with the collective spirit of team spirit she had helped domesticate.

For Rachel, the Mystic Seeker, changed into not only a lone hero, but a image of a collective dream. A dream of expertise, collaboration, and a destiny where the interconnected realms, sure by means of shared reviews and cause, could all the time stand, a beacon of desire in opposition to the encroaching darkness.

CHAPTER TEN

Takeaways

1.   Unity   is   Power: Facing   seemingly insurmountable   challenges   requires   collective strength.   Building   bridges   across   differences, fostering empathy, and working towards a common goal can achieve what individuals cannot.

2. Understanding Breeds Harmony: Fear and prejudice stem from a lack of understanding. Open communication, cultural exchange, and celebrating diversity   pave   the   way   for   acceptance   and collaboration.

3. Hope is a Weapon: Even in the face of despair, clinging to hope and fostering positivity can be the most potent weapon. It fuels resilience, inspires action, and weakens the grip of negativity.

4. Knowledge is Key: Seeking ancient wisdom, forgotten lore, and diverse perspectives equips us to face challenges and chart a brighter future. Curiosity and collaboration unlock the potential for innovation and progress.

5. Leadership Requires Empathy: True leadership transcends authority. It demands understanding the needs   and   fears   of   others,   fostering   trust,   and inspiring collective action through shared purpose.

6. The Journey Never Ends: Even after achieving milestones,   challenges   remain.   Embrace   the continuous journey of exploration, adaptation, and collaboration to ensure lasting peace and progress.

7. Every Individual Matters: Even a single seeker, driven by purpose and compassion, can ignite change. Recognize the potential within yourself and others to contribute to a better future.

Remember: This story is a tapestry woven from imagination and hope. Let its lessons inspire you to build bridges, embrace understanding, and contribute to a more harmonious world, wherever you may find yourself.

Epilogue

Years after the Nexus Project's inception, whispers of another threat began to stir. This time, the danger manifested not from a cosmic entity, but from within. Whispers of dissent, fueled by isolationist sentiments and resource scarcity, threatened to fracture the hard-earned unity.

Rachel, older now but her spirit undimmed, faced this new challenge with the wisdom earned on her long journey. She reminded the realms of their shared history, the perils overcome, and the strength found in collaboration. She initiated the "Harmony Exchange," a program fostering deeper cultural understanding and resource sharing, addressing the root causes of discontent.

Acknowledgements:

The chronicler of this saga owes a debt of gratitude to the following:

The vibrant imagination of countless readers who fueled the journey with their engagement and support.

The boundless creativity of fellow storytellers whose works inspired and challenged the narrative's exploration.

The unwavering belief in the power of stories to shape minds and hearts, a belief that kept the pen moving and the tale unfolding.

Further Exploration:

This story concludes, but the universe of Rachel, the Mystic Seeker, holds countless untold tales. Explore additional stories and delve deeper into:

The adventures of individual characters from across the interconnected realms.

Untold chapters of the Nexus Project, uncovering hidden dangers and wondrous discoveries.

The rise and fall of civilizations, exploring the lessons learned and the echoes they leave behind.

Remember, dear reader, the story may end, but the journey of understanding, collaboration, and hope continues. Carry the spark ignited by Rachel's tale within you, and weave your own thread into the grand tapestry of existence.